☆ ☆ ☆ ☆ ☆

My other books are amazingly amazing too!

'Made me laugh out loud. Ellie May rocks!' Andy Stanton, author of *Mr Gum*

'...l poke at the fame game . . . packed with wit and lively illustrations.'
Independent on Sunday

'I loved Ellie May. There wasn't a page I didn't like - it was
sooooooo good!' Imogen, age 9

'...perbly quirky and amusing.' Konnie Huq (Blue Peter, The Xtra Factor)

'...ought this book was amazing and a real page-turner.' Grace, age 8

'Move...ver, Clarice Bean! A wonderful read for young fashionistas!' *Carousel*

'Oh...here comes Ellie May! She had me choking on my fudge cake with
laughter!' Mel Giedroyc (The Great British Bake Off)

'...lenty of laugh-out-loud moments. Ellie May is a heroine with
attitude a go-go.'

'I wo...like Ellie May to come to my sch...
I giggled so much reading it I f...

'...e May is very funny. This is serious...
Poppy, age 8

'Vivacious and hilarious.' *The Bookseller*

'I loved this book more than fudge cake.' Freya, age 8

'Girls will love this new heroine and laugh out loud at her antics.'
Angels and Urchins

'Fast, daft and funny. You're guaranteed unalloyed hilarity!'

To Kevin, my very own Jeffrey

EGMONT
We bring stories to life

Ellie May Can Definitely be
Trusted to Keep a Secret
First published in paperback in Great Britain
2013 by Jelly Pie, an imprint of
Egmont UK Limited
The Yellow Building, 1 Nicholas Road
London W11 4AN

Text copyright © 2013 Marianne Levy
Illustrations copyright © 2013 Ali Pye

The moral rights of the author and illustrator
have been asserted

ISBN 978 1 4052 6662 8
3 5 7 9 10 8 6 4 2

www.egmont.co.uk
www.jellypiecentral.co.uk

A CIP catalogue record for this title is
available from the British Library

54741/3

Printed and bound in Great Britain by the
CPI Group

EGMONT

MIX
Paper
FSC FSC® C018306

ELLIE MAY

Can Definitely be Trusted to Keep a Secret

Marianne Levy

EGMONT

Contents

Chapter One

Ellie May Can Definitely be Trusted to Keep a Secret

'Are we nearly there yet?' asked Ellie May. 'I know I asked five minutes ago but I sort of hope we might have somehow jumped forwards in time and also I've been talking for a while now so that probably took a few more minutes and anyway I'm just wondering, are we nearly there?'

'Why don't you read a magazine or something?' asked Jeffrey. 'Or play the game where you don't say anything for as long as possible? See if you can beat your record of nine seconds.'

'I would do,' sighed Ellie May, 'but it's impossible. I don't think anyone's ever been quiet for that long. Unless they're dead. And that's against the rules.'

Ellie May was an incredibly famous film star. She was so famous that there were handbags decorated with her initials. There were sweatshirts printed with her face. And a chef in Paris had just invented 'Ellie May Tomatoes'.

Today, she was sitting on a plane to New York, where she would soon do a TV interview for her latest film. Her chaperone, Jeffrey, sat in the next seat, reading, while Ellie May flipped through a magazine.

'What about now?' asked Ellie May. 'I bet we're nearly there now. Are we? Jeffrey? Are we? Because I'm so so so so *so* bored.'

Jeffrey looked up from his book. 'Count the seats on the plane,' he said.

'I have. There are exactly four hundred,' said Ellie May.

'Number of people wearing glasses?' asked Jeffrey.

'A hundred and eighty-two,' said Ellie May. 'And there are thirty-four people with beards. Thirty-three men and one surprisingly hairy lady.'

'*Giggle* looks very interesting this week,' said Jeffrey. 'Have you read the interview with Cassie Craven?'

Ellie May turned the page.

CASSIE CRAVEN'S FINAL INTERVIEW

Cassie Craven's just announced that she's not doing any more interviews! Yes, the beautiful blonde starlet is stepping out of the limelight once and for all.

'I'm just fed up of people sticking their noses into my personal life,' she told us. 'That's the problem with going on TV and being in magazines. You never get any privacy. I don't want people asking me questions and taking photos; it makes me really uncomfortable. Now, would you like to come and see my new trampoline? And bring your camera. It's purple!'

5

'There's one in *Dazzle* too,' said Jeffrey,

opening the magazine to the headline:

CASSIE CRAVEN STOPS TALKING

'No more interviews for me,' Cassie Craven told our showbiz correspondent . . .

'And she's in *Kisses*,' said Ellie May.

LAST WORDS FROM CASSIE CRAVEN

'This really is it,' said Cassie, as she sipped a strawberry juice . . .

'Why wouldn't she want to be interviewed?' pondered Ellie May. 'I love everyone knowing all about me. That's why I did that documentary, *Ellie May's Amazing Days*. Are we nearly there yet?'

'Not yet,' said Jeffrey. 'Why don't you sit and think fascinating thoughts?'

'I haven't got any fascinating thoughts,' said Ellie May. 'Not even one.'

'Oh, come on,' said Jeffrey. 'We both know that you have a very lively imagination.'

'No I haven't,' said Ellie May. 'I can't think of anything at all right now except one small grey pebble. Bor-ing.'

'Well, would you like some fudge cake?' tried Jeffrey. 'Or a lovely long, long, long, long sleep?'

'Maybe a piece of fudge cake,' said Ellie May.

'You could play the game of seeing how quietly you can eat it,' suggested Jeffrey, handing Ellie May her plate.

'Yes!' said Ellie May. 'Wait. No. That's not an official game.'

'Isn't it?' asked Jeffrey wearily.

'Nope,' said Ellie May. 'Not like piggy-in-the-middle. Or hide-and-cake. I hope they do fudge cake at our hotel. Where is that, by the way? And are we nearly there yet?'

'Nearer than we were, thank goodness,' said Jeffrey. 'It's called The Hotel Splendido Marvellousa and it's brand new. It does sound pretty splendid, actually. There's a swimming pool and a spa and three different restaurants. They're trying to get lots of celebrities to stay there. In fact . . . actually, nothing.'

'What?' asked Ellie May.

'Nothing,' said Jeffrey.

'Nothing?' said Ellie May.

'Nothing,' said Jeffrey.

'Nothing what?' asked Ellie May.

'Nothing nothing,' said Jeffrey.

'If it's nothing then why did you say it was nothing?' asked Ellie May slyly.

'What?' said Jeffrey.

'Exactly,' said Ellie May. 'What?!'

'OK, OK, there's someone quite exciting staying at the hotel with us,' admitted Jeffrey. 'But I'm not allowed to tell you who it is, so don't ask me.'

Ellie May ate a bit of fudge cake. Then she ate a bit more fudge cake. 'This is very nice fudge cake, Jeffrey,' she said. 'It's particularly delicious and I wonder what the recipe was by the way who's staying with us and would you like a piece?'

'You can't catch me out that easily,' said Jeffrey. 'And I'm not telling you because you are awful at keeping secrets.'

'That is *not true*!' cried Ellie May. 'I can definitely be trusted to keep a secret!'

'Good,' said Jeffrey. 'Now, are you going to finish that?'

'Maybe in a bit,' said Ellie May. 'I'm not as hungry as I was.' She sniffed.

'Are you sure?' asked Jeffrey.

Ellie May sniffed again, and dabbed her eyes with a corner of her collar. 'You just read your book, Jeffrey. Don't worry about me.'

'Oh, all right, all right,' sighed Jeffrey. 'But look, you really do have to promise not to tell.'

'I completely promise,' said Ellie May. 'Now, who is it?'

'It's Kiko,' said Jeffrey. 'But –'

'I CAN'T BELIEVE THAT KIKO IS STAYING IN THE SAME HOTEL AS US!' shouted Ellie May. 'I KNOW YOU SAID THE HOTEL SPLENDIDO MARVELLOUSA WOULD BE SPLENDID, BUT THIS IS MARVELLOUS. IN FACT, IT'S MARVELLOUSA! HOORAY! HOORAY! HOO–'

'Shhhhhhh!' hissed Jeffrey. 'You said . . . you promised . . .'

The man behind them leaned in between the seats. 'Kiko?' he asked. 'As in the ultra-famous-multi-Oscar-winning-number-one-album-selling superstar? *That* Kiko?'

'Ellie May . . .' began Jeffrey.

The woman in the seat in front turned round, a huge smile spreading across her hairy face.

'I love Kiko! I've got all her books!'

'I can't believe she's in New York!' exclaimed a nearby flight attendant.

'Oh, Ellie May,' moaned Jeffrey.

'Good evening, ladies and gentlemen.' The voice of the captain came over the tannoy. 'We'll shortly be landing in New York City. The time is twenty-two minutes past six, the temperature is a pleasant seventy-one degrees, and I've just heard that Kiko is staying at The Hotel Splendido Marvellousa. Please return your seats to the upright position . . .'

Jeffrey put his head in his hands.

'Sorry,' whispered Ellie May.

'I trusted you,' said Jeffrey.

'I know,' said Ellie May.

'Supposing I told everyone all your secrets?' asked Jeffrey. 'I could stand up right now and tell the whole plane about the incident with the candyfloss. Is that what you want, Ellie May? Is it?'

'No,' said Ellie May, wishing she could stuff the words back into her mouth again. 'I'm really and truly sorry. I do want to be able to keep secrets as well as you. How do you do it?'

'I just do,' said Jeffrey crossly. 'Now put your seat belt on. We're landing in a minute.'

15

Ellie May clicked her seat belt together. From now on she'd keep every secret perfectly. People would trust her so much that they'd probably come to her with things that they just couldn't tell other, ordinary people. She smiled.

'Don't worry, Jeffrey,' she said. 'I've decided that I'm going to be the best person at keeping secrets that ever lived. And I'm sure everyone will have forgotten about Kiko already. I mean, it's not like people are even *that* interested in her. Is it?'

The Hotel Splendido Marvellousa stood at the top of a flight of beautiful marble steps. At least, it probably did. In fact, the steps could have been made of cheddar cheese as far as Ellie May could tell, because they were completely covered with people.

'Excuse me,' said Ellie May, stepping round a man clutching Kiko's new album.

'If I could just get through . . .' said Jeffrey, pushing past a woman holding Kiko's latest novel.

'KIKO! KIKO! KIKO!' chanted a group of schoolchildren, who were all dressed up as Kiko.

Ellie May sauntered over. 'Hello,' she said.

'I'm staying here too. You've probably heard of me. I'm –'

'Ellie May!' gasped the nearest girl. She held out an autograph book. 'Can you –'

'Of course,' said Ellie May, feeling in her bag for a pen.

'– give this to Kiko?' asked the girl. 'Tell her to sign it "To Beth". Thanks.'

'Um, all right,' said Ellie May, taking the book.

'Oh, *LOOK*!' shrieked the girl. 'It's Kiko's spokesman!'

A man wearing a dark suit and a frown stepped through the hotel doors into the sunshine.

The shouts died down as everyone listened.

'Good evening, everyone, I am Kiko's spokesman,' said Kiko's spokesman. 'I speak on behalf of Kiko, and I would like to inform you . . .'

The man with the album leaned in. The woman with the novel crossed her fingers.

'. . . that . . .'

The schoolgirl held her breath.

'. . . Kiko . . .'

A squirrel just carried on as usual.

'. . . will not be making a statement at this time. Thank you.'

Then he turned and went back inside.

Jeffrey picked up his suitcase.

'Let's get checked in to our rooms,' he said.

'But someone might want my autograph,' protested Ellie May.

'You can give your autograph to the man who carries our bags,' said Jeffrey. 'Come on, Ellie May.'

Ellie May's suite in The Hotel Splendido Marvellousa was as splendidly marvellous as it was marvellously splendid.

The walls were covered with mirrors and

the sofa was covered with cushions. A chandelier covered the ceiling with splashes of golden light and the room-service menu was covered with a silver cover.

The bed was king-sized, which meant that it was big enough for a king. Kings, Ellie May knew, are actually the same size as normal people, but they do like to sleep in particularly large beds.

Ellie May wandered into the bathroom and peered at the bath. Instead of taps, there was a single lever, and next to it was a small plaque inscribed with the words:

> **Pull this lever to run a hot bath in less than one minute!**
>
> # DO NOT LEAVE BATH UNATTENDED

Ellie May pulled the lever, and then picked up the room-service menu. She was just choosing between several different types of milkshake when her phone started ringing.

'Hello!' said Jeffrey. 'How's your room? I think I'm directly underneath you.'

'Jeffrey!' cried Ellie May. 'My room's amazingly amazing!'

'Mine too,' said Jeffrey. 'I seem to have three televisions! This hotel is extraordinary. Are you all unpacked? Can I come up?'

'In a minute,' said Ellie May. 'I'm just running myself a lovely bath.'

'Well, call me when you've finished,' said Jeffrey. 'We must have a chat about your TV interview.'

'And we've got to order from room service,' said Ellie May. 'They have a milkshake that tastes like popcorn! *And* one that tastes of hamburgers. No, wait, that's a hamburger. Oooh, look, they do fudge cake! It's got fudge icing and pieces of fudge inside and triple-fudge sauce. And they serve it on a plate made of fudge! Can I have some, Jeffrey?

Can I? Can I?'

'You can have some tomorrow . . .' Jeffrey began. 'Hmm. That's odd.'

'What's odd?' asked Ellie May.

'There seems to be water coming through my ceiling,' said Jeffrey.

'Really?' asked Ellie May.

'Yes,' said Jeffrey. 'Quite a lot of water, in fact.'

'You should complain,' said Ellie May. 'It's very bad that such a nice hotel would have water coming through the – aaaaaaargh!'

'Hello?' called Jeffrey. 'Are you all right? Hello?'

Ellie May ran to her bathroom, which was now mainly bath.

'Oh dear,' she said.

There was a sharp knock.

'Jeffrey?' called Ellie May. She opened the door.

'Hi, sorry, I was just looking for . . . Oh!'

Standing in the doorway was a lean boy, about the same age as Ellie May, with shaggy blond hair and long legs. He was wearing a floppy red tracksuit with the word STAR across the front, and his teeth were a bright and glossy white.

'Hey, you're Ellie May!' cried the boy. 'High five?'

After a moment, Ellie May reached out to his hand and shook it.

'Hello,' she said graciously. 'Would you like my autograph? Who should I make it out to?'

'I'm Zack-short-for-Zachary-but-everyone-calls-me-Zack,' said the boy. 'But I don't want your –'

'It's very nice to meet you,' said Ellie May. 'Is that Zack spelled Z-A-C-K?'

'Seriously, don't worry about it,' said Zack. 'I was actually looking for Kiko.'

'Oh,' said Ellie May. 'Right. Fine. But you could still get my autograph, since you're here? I'll do you a really pretty one with a little star on it and everything.'

A man in uniform appeared behind him. 'Excuse me. Was that your bath that overflowed just now? We've had some complaints.'

'Sorry,' said Ellie May. 'Oooh, would you like my autograph too? You'll have to form a queue because there's someone else waiting, but don't worry, I'll get to everyone eventually.'

'Er, no, thank you,' said the man. 'And I'll have to ask you to step outside for a few minutes while we mop up. Would you like to wait downstairs?'

Ellie May grinned at Zack. 'It's OK,' she said. 'I'm going to wait with – what did you say your name was?'

'Zack,' said Zack. 'But . . .'

To Z-A-C-K,

wrote Ellie May.

My number one fan!
Hugs, Ellie May x

Chapter Two

Ellie May Doesn't Want to Sing a Top Q

Jeffrey came out of the lift just in time to see Ellie
May's handbag swing past as she raced away.

'Wait!' he called. 'I thought we were going to
talk about your TV interview!'

Ellie May spun around. 'Sorry, Jeffrey, I can't
right now,' she explained. 'I've got plans with Zack.'

'Really?' said Jeffrey.

'Yes,' said Ellie May. 'He's a big fan of mine.'

'No I'm not,' said Zack.

'Yes, you are,' said Ellie May. 'You just haven't realised it yet.'

Jeffrey nodded. 'All right,' he said. 'Make sure you stay in the hotel, Ellie May, and I'll see you later.'

Ellie May darted off around the corner. Jeffrey waited a moment, and then shrugged. The corridor of The Splendido Marvellousa stretched out long and empty before him. He had the hotel all to himself.

What should he do first?

Jeffrey tucked his book under his arm and ambled back to the lift, where there hung a sign which said:

LUXURY SPA & POOL	floor 0
LUXURY RESTAURANT	floor 1
LUXURY RELAXATION ZONE	floor 7
LUXURY ENERGY ZONE	floor 8
LUXURY LUXURY ZONE	floor 11
OTHER LUXURY RESTAURANT	floor 14
EXTRA SURPRISE SUPER LUXURY RESTAURANT	floor 25
LUXURY THE ROOF	floor 26

'Hmm,' murmured Jeffrey, his eyes darting back and forth across the curly gold lettering. 'Maybe the Luxury Relaxation Zone would be . . . Oh! Hello!'

A thin, serious man with a thin, serious nose was studying the sign, too. He looked like the very opposite of a funfair.

'I recognise you,' said Jeffrey. 'Aren't you . . . now, hold on . . . give me a second . . . I'll get it . . . sorry, I'm a bit tired . . . nearly there . . . it's on the tip of my tongue . . . you're . . . you're Kiko's spokesman! Phew! Nice to meet you.'

'You too,' said Kiko's spokesman, shaking Jeffrey's hand. 'So, what brings you here?'

'I'm Ellie May's chaperone,' said Jeffrey. 'Which is not ever so different from being a spokesman, I imagine. Except that with Ellie May it's the opposite. I don't say things for her – I have to *stop* her saying things. She likes to tell everyone everything. It can be . . . awkward.'

Kiko's spokesman nodded. 'I can imagine,' he said.

'It's worse than you can imagine,' said Jeffrey.

They smiled.

'I was just heading to the Relaxation Zone,' said Kiko's spokesman. 'Would you care to join me? It would be good to have some company.'

'Yes, please,' said Jeffrey. 'This is a marvellous hotel, but I'm finding it all a bit overwhelming. Too much carpet, I think. And everything's shiny and twiddly. I just want to sit down somewhere quiet and have a nice read before bed.' Jeffrey reached out to press the lift button and his book fell to the floor. 'This is one of Kiko's, actually. Did it take her very long to write?'

Kiko's spokesman froze. 'I have no statement to make about Kiko at this time,' he said.

'Oh, right,' said Jeffrey. 'Just . . . she must be so busy with her films and her music, I only wondered whether –'

35

'I have no statement to make about Kiko at this time,' said Kiko's spokesman.

'I really wasn't trying to, you know, find out stuff,' said Jeffrey. 'I'd hate it if you thought I was just after information. Kiko's life is nothing to do with me.'

'I have no statement to make about Kiko at this time,' repeated Kiko's spokesman.

Jeffrey drew himself up as tall as he could, and gave his bow tie a little tweak. 'Well, in that case,' he said haughtily, 'I have no statement to make about Ellie May, either. So there. I hope you have a very relaxing evening. I shall be spending mine

elsewhere.' The lift doors opened. 'Up or down?'

'I have no statement to make at this time,' said Kiko's spokesman.

'Me neither,' said Jeffrey. 'But, um, floor eight? Actually, I think I'll take the stairs.'

Ellie May followed Zack as he spun up and down the corridor.

'Kiko's definitely not on this floor,' he said. 'I've checked. Shall we try the next one?'

'All right,' said Ellie May. 'I'll go first and you can stand behind me.'

'Why?' asked Zack. 'I want to go first. It was my idea!'

'I know, but I'm the incredibly famous one, not you,' said Ellie May kindly. 'And Kiko's incredibly famous too, so we have lots in common.'

'Do you know her, then?' asked Zack.

'Not especially,' said Ellie May. 'But I know lots of other celebrities. Lots and lots and lots. Hey, you dropped your autograph!'

Zack turned around and put his hands on his hips. 'Well, actually,' he said, 'I'm famous too. I'm in a Broadway show!'

'That's lovely,' said Ellie May. 'Anyway . . .'

'On Broadway!' said Zack.

Ellie May shrugged.

'You do know what I'm talking about, don't you?' said Zack.

'No,' said Ellie May. 'Is it like a dog show?'

'No, it's a musical show,' said Zack. 'And Broadway shows are the best musicals in the world. I'm going to be singing and dancing, and outside the theatre they've written my name in lights!'

'Well, I'm in films,' said Ellie May. 'Loads and loads of films. I did a film about Broadway once. Oh, no, hang on, it was about a broad *bean*. Still, though . . .'

'You know what?' said Zack crossly. 'I think I might go and look for Kiko on my own.'

'What will you say when you find her?' asked Ellie May, following Zack past a machine that dispensed ice and a machine that dispensed cups for ice and a machine that didn't dispense anything because it was a clock.

'I'm going to tell her that I think she's incredible,' said Zack. 'I'll get her to sign a photo of herself, and I'll sign one of me in return and I'll ask her whether she'd like a part in my show. Or we can talk about doing an album together. And then I'll show her my somersaults.'

'You can sign a

photograph for me if you like,'

said Ellie May generously. 'I won't mind.'

Zack twizzled around and around. 'Hey, do

you like my pirouettes? I can do them for ages

42

before I get dizzy. Once I did forty in a row. My dance teacher gave me a prize.'

'A prize like an award?' asked Ellie May. 'I've won lots of those.'

'But I bet you've never won one for your pirouettes, like I have,' said Zack.

'I haven't, no,' said Ellie May. 'But I did win an award for best celebrity hair last week. That's why the hotel invited me to stay. Not because of my hair, although it is nice. Because I'm so incredibly famous.'

'They invited me to stay here specially too,' said Zack, spinning on the spot like a demented egg whisk. 'And *I* get five-star treatment. When I went to breakfast today I was allowed as many waffles as I wanted and if I get lonely I can call reception and they'll send me up a goldfish.'

'Why?' asked Ellie May.

'To be my friend,' said Zack.

Ellie May beamed at Zack. 'Well, you don't need a goldfish now,' she said, 'because *I'm* your friend. There! Isn't that great? You must be so happy. I don't make friends with just anyone, you know.'

Zack lifted his chin. 'You can audition to be my friend, if you like.'

'Audition?' repeated Ellie May.

44

'Yes,' said Zack. 'I don't make friends with just anyone, either.'

Ellie May nodded. 'All right,' she said. 'What do I have to do?'

Zack slowed to a halt, a strange smile spreading across his sharp little face. 'Let's start with a bit of movement. Are you warmed up?'

'I'm all right,' said Ellie May. 'I can put on a coat, if you want me to be even warmer.'

'You can't do the splits in a coat!' snorted Zack.

'Actually, I can't do the splits at all,' admitted Ellie May.

'Oh dear,' said Zack. 'This audition isn't going very well. But I suppose it's cool, so long as you're good at jazz and modern.'

'Modern what?' said Ellie May.

Zack flicked his hair out of his eyes. 'You may be famous but you don't seem to be very talented,' he said. 'Let's move on to singing. What's your range?'

'My what?' said Ellie May, who was starting to feel a bit less friendly than before.

'Your vocal range,' said Zack. 'I can sing a Top C. *Laaa!*'

'Well . . . in that case . . . I can sing a Top Q,' said Ellie May.

'There isn't a Top Q,' said Zack. 'You just made it up.'

'Just because you've never heard of it, doesn't mean there isn't one,' snapped Ellie May. 'Probably I'm a more advanced singer than you are.'

Zack folded his arms. 'All right then,' he said. 'Sing a Top Q now.'

Ellie May felt her eyes start to sting. 'I don't want to sing a Top Q,' she said. 'Anyway, incredibly famous film stars don't need to sing. Even though obviously I absolutely can.'

'No you can't,' said Zack.

'I can,' said Ellie May. 'You're just being mean

because you've never been in a film and I've been in lots and lots and lots and lots.'

'Well, *you're* just being mean because you've never been in a Broadway show,' said Zack. 'And I don't think you ever will be, either. Not if you do an audition like that.'

Ellie May turned away. 'I'm going to get back to my room now,' she said.

Zack peered at her. 'You're not . . . you're not crying, are you?'

'I really really have to go,' quavered Ellie May, feeling herself getting hotter and redder by the second. 'I've got some very important

48

things to do. Because I'm going on television on Friday night. Actual television!'

'Television isn't really my thing,' said Zack. 'My director always says that it's entertainment for stupid people.'

'Then . . . then . . . *you're* stupid,' said Ellie May, opening her bedroom door.

Zack chuckled. 'Sorry, Ellie May, but you have failed your audition. Better luck next time.'

'Fine,' said Ellie May. 'Have fun practising your banana splits. Goodnight.'

Back in her room, Ellie May clambered up on to her bed and stared at the ceiling.

The ceiling stared back.

'I'm *very* talented,' said Ellie May. 'I'm an incredibly famous film star.'

The ceiling wasn't very impressed.

Ellie May tried singing a Top Q. It didn't sound particularly nice. Then she jumped off the bed and had a go at spinning a pirouette. It was quite good, until she fell into the wardrobe.

She looked around the room for something to cheer herself up. The room looked back, shiny and perfect and silent.

Ellie May shivered. Maybe she'd go for a swim. Or a walk. Or a waffle. She opened the door and slipped out into the corridor.

But this was even worse. If Ellie May's room had felt empty, then the rest of the hotel was as deserted as a dessert table that had run out of dessert.

Jeffrey must have gone to bed, because although she knocked and knocked, there was no reply.

The restaurants were shut.

The spa was closed.

The Relaxation Zone wasn't even there,

because Ellie May had gone to the wrong floor.

Ellie May walked and walked, Zack's words going round and round her head.

'You can't dance,' whispered the ice dispenser.

'You can't sing,' crooned the cup dispenser.

'Tick-tock,' cackled the clock.

Ellie May walked and walked until there was only one place left to go.

Out on the roof, a cold wind whipped through Ellie May's hair and chilled the tears that ran down her cheeks.

'Are you all right?'

The voice was soft and kind.

'No,' sobbed Ellie May. 'I don't think I am.'

A hand brushed her shoulder, and Ellie May looked up to see a woman peering down at her. A beautiful woman, with large, dark, worried eyes. She was so rare and lovely that she looked as if she might vanish at any moment, like a snowflake in the sunshine.

'Please don't cry,' she said.

Ellie May's mouth dropped open, and when she spoke, her voice was just a whisper. 'I can't . . . I don't . . . you're . . . you must be . . .'

'Kiko,' said Kiko.

Chapter Three

Ellie May Feels an Awful Lot Happier Now

'I recognise you, don't I?' said Kiko. 'You're Ellie May!'

Ellie May nodded, and snuffled.

'And you're upset,' said Kiko. 'You can't sit out here on your own. Why aren't you in your room?'

'. . . too . . . lonely . . .' managed Ellie May.

Kiko nodded. 'I know,' she said. 'There's nothing more miserable than an empty hotel room, is there?' She shivered. 'But we'd better not stay out here. Look, why don't we go down to my suite? Two film stars together! And then you can blow your nose and tell me what happened.' She took Ellie May's hand and led her back inside.

A small, plain door stood tucked behind the stairs to the roof. Kiko knocked twice, waited a moment, and then opened it, waving Ellie May inside. 'Here we are.'

Ellie May stared and stared and stared.

As an incredibly famous film star staying at The Hotel Splendido Marvellousa, Ellie May had an incredibly lovely room.

But Kiko was an incredibly fantastically astonishingly famous star, and her room was like nothing Ellie May had ever seen before. And Ellie May had seen most things, including a mango attacking a tiger in her hit movie *Soft Fruit Bites Back*.

Not one but three emperor-sized beds sat side by side, looking out across New York. Emperors, Ellie May knew, like to have bigger beds than kings, even though actually emperors and kings are generally about the same size. The floor was clad with a thick layer of deep purple velvet and the ceiling was scattered with little lights, which sparkled like diamonds, or stars, or stars covered with diamonds and then fitted with tiny light bulbs.

'Is that the Empire Snake Building?' asked Ellie May.

'It's the Empire *State* Building,' said Kiko.

'That's what I said,' replied Ellie May, stepping round a corner and –

'Careful!' cried Kiko.

– nearly falling into a swimming pool.

'Are you all right?' asked Kiko.

'You have an actual swimming pool in your actual room!' squealed Ellie May.

'Well,' said Kiko, looking a tiny bit awkward, 'I don't really like to swim in front of other people. I prefer to be . . . private. Otherwise the papers would be full of articles called things like "Kiko's Lucky Dip" and "Kiko's Day is Going Swimmingly". Ugh.' She shuddered.

'Yes. Completely ugh,' agreed Ellie May, who rather liked it when people tried to take pictures of her, but somehow knew that this was not really what Kiko wanted to hear.

'I just hate everyone prying into my personal

life all the time,' said Kiko.

'Me too,' said Ellie May. 'It's dreadfully dreadful.'

'And so unfair,' Kiko sighed. 'Why do people need to know everything about me?'

'Mmm,' said Ellie May, hoping that Kiko hadn't read last week's *Giggle*, with its cover story,

EVERYTHING ABOUT ME
by Ellie May

'Now,' said Kiko, sitting down on one of the beds. 'Why were you crying?'

Ellie May remembered Zack's scornful voice. 'It's . . . there was . . . I met this b-boy just now, he's in this show, on Broadway, and he was m-mean to me . . . because I can't tap-dance or sing a Top Q. I thought I was quite g-g-good at being a film star, but now I know that I'm not actually very good after all.' Ellie May tried to wipe away the tears before Kiko could see them, but there were so many that she knew she must have missed some.

'That's horrible,' said Kiko. 'Why are people so cruel? But we'll get it sorted out. Now, are you hungry? I've got some chocolate chip cookies. Would a cookie make you feel better?'

'I think it might,' admitted Ellie May.

'Now, look,' said Kiko, passing Ellie May a brand new packet of very expensive biscuits. 'About what that awful boy said. He's just jealous, Ellie May.'

'I suppose so,' said Ellie May. 'But it doesn't change anything. I can't dance very well. And I really can't sing. Not like you can.'

Kiko fiddled with the hem of her skirt. 'I don't think it matters whether I can sing or not. What's important is that –'

'But it does!' cried Ellie May. 'That's the *whole point*! You're this amazingly incredible actress who wins all these awards and you dance better than anyone and you write whole entire books and even Jeffrey's got one of your albums and he normally listens to boring old people's music. So I'm very sorry, Kiko, because you're totally lovely, but talking to you has sort of made me feel even worse. I think next time I ought to speak to someone rubbishy and untalented. Like m-m-m-me.' Ellie May burst into loud sobs.

Kiko gasped. 'Please don't cry,' she said. 'No one can do everything!'

'You can!' howled Ellie May.

'I'm really not as good as you say,' cried Kiko.

'Yes, you are,' wept Ellie May.

'I'm *really* not,' said Kiko. She watched as tear after tear slid down Ellie May's unhappy cheeks.

And then Kiko got to her feet. 'Look,' she said. 'I'm going to tell you something no one else knows. Something that I think might help you feel a lot better.'

Ellie May blew her nose on a very expensive tissue, and waited.

'I'm . . . I'm not quite what you think I am,' said Kiko. 'I mean, I am. But, also, I'm not. Do you know what I mean?'

'No,' said Ellie May.

'OK,' said Kiko. 'I'll try again. I *am* good at acting. Very good. I love acting. But when it comes to singing and dancing, I'm hopeless. I don't have any kind of talent at all. I've tried, goodness knows. I've worked and worked, but I just don't have it in me.'

Ellie May frowned. 'Then how come you're so amazing in all your music videos?' she asked. 'And your concerts? I've seen you sing and dance lots of times.'

'I was amazing because . . . because . . .' Kiko got to her feet, went to a door and knocked, slowly and deliberately, five times. After a moment, it opened, and a woman stepped out.

A beautiful woman, with large, dark eyes.

A woman identical to Kiko.

'I was amazing because it wasn't me,' said Kiko. 'Ellie May, this is my twin sister, Katsu. Katsu, this is Ellie May.'

'Hello, Ellie May,' said Katsu.

Ellie May's head swung from Kiko to Katsu
and back again.

'*What?*' she gasped. 'You're two people at the
same time? That's literally not possible.'

'I only ever wanted to act,' said Kiko. 'But in my first movie, way before I was famous, there was this big song-and-dance number. And I told the director that I could do it because I wanted the part so much. Then filming got closer and closer and I couldn't bear to tell him that I couldn't do it. So on the day we did that scene, I stayed at home and Katsu pretended to be me. And then the film was a huge hit and I got my first award and . . . well, I just kept doing it.'

'*We* got *our* first award,' said Katsu.

'That's what I meant,' said Kiko.

'But why didn't you tell anyone after that?'

68

asked Ellie May.

'Because it would have been such a huge scandal,' said Katsu. 'Kiko has it bad enough right now, with reporters stalking her day and night.'

Kiko nodded. 'I don't know how they found out I'm staying here – I swore everyone to secrecy. Apparently the rumours came from the airport, which is weird, because . . . Ellie May, are you all right? You've gone a very funny colour. Oh dear, you're choking!'

'Blwaaaa!' coughed Ellie May, spraying guilty biscuit crumbs across the bedclothes. 'Sorry.

Oh dear. Ahem.' She swallowed. 'But how come no one's ever found out about you, Katsu?'

'We hardly ever go out in public together,' said Katsu. 'And when we do, I have to wear glasses. And fake tan and make-up and a bright-pink wig. And sometimes a fat suit, just to be sure.'

'A pink wig sounds fun,' said Ellie May. 'Can I try it on?'

'It's not fun, it's awful,' said Katsu. 'Kiko's followed wherever she goes and I'm basically invisible. Even when I go out and sing to a whole stadium full of people, Kiko gets the credit!'

'You never told me you felt like that,' said

Kiko sharply. 'Why didn't you tell me?'

'I'm telling you now,' said Katsu.

'But the photographers, people watching me all the time and talking about me, being in the newspaper every time I pick my nose or go for a coffee,' said Kiko. 'You're so lucky, Katsu. You don't have to put up with any of that.'

'I wouldn't mind,' said Katsu. 'I think I'd enjoy it. I'm not you, Kiko. And I'm sick of pretending that I am.'

'Well, I'm sorry, but it's too late,' said Kiko.

Katsu held her sister's gaze. 'Maybe,' she said softly. 'Or maybe not.'

Ellie May's phone beeped.

> Are you OK? Sorry, I went to the Luxury Energy Zone and fell asleep. It isn't a very energetic place after all. Jeffrey

'I'd better go,' said Ellie May. 'But thank you, Kiko. And Katsu. I feel an awful lot happier now. And I will try to remember what you said. I'll try really hard.'

Katsu hesitated for a moment, then she reached out and took Ellie May's phone. 'Smile!' she said. The phone flashed, and she spun it round.

There, on the screen, was a picture of Ellie
May and Katsu and Kiko.

'The three of us, together,' said Katsu. 'Next
time you get upset, just
look at this and remember
our chat. It'll be OK,
Ellie May.'

'Katsu!' cried Kiko.
'I can't believe you
did that! You know
the rule! No photos
of the two us
together. *EVER*.'

Katsu put her arm around her sister. 'Don't worry. I trust Ellie May. She won't show anyone.'

'Of course I won't. You can definitely trust me,' said Ellie May.

Jeffrey paced up and down and up and down the hotel corridor. And, after a bit, a lithe blond figure came cartwheeling past him.

'Excuse me!' called Jeffrey. 'I don't suppose you've seen Ellie May? Wasn't she with you, just now? It's just, she's not in her room and I'm her chaperone, you see, so I need to make sure she's not gone midnight shopping. Again.'

'She's not with me,' said Zack. 'She went off about half an hour ago. I'm Zack-short-for-Zachary-but-everyone-calls-me-Zack and I'm in a Broadway show!'

'Right. Great,' said Jeffrey. 'Did she . . . did she say when she was coming back?'

'Nope,' said Zack. 'Do you want to see my routine? The show opens on Saturday so I need to rehearse.'

'Um, all right,' said Jeffrey.

'High five!' cried Zack. 'I haven't done it to a grown-up yet. I'll pretend I'm not just practising in the hotel. You're the audience and I'm on the stage, on Broadway!'

'OK,' said Jeffrey. 'So, you're behind the curtain. You can hear everyone sitting down and talking and reading about you in the programme. The music starts and all those hundreds of people go quiet, and everyone's watching the stage, waiting for you to come and show them what you've got.'

Zack gulped.

'And then,' said Jeffrey encouragingly, 'you're standing under the hot, bright lights and all those faces are looking at you, staring at you, and . . .'

Zack began to shake.

'And?' prompted Jeffrey.

Zack scrunched his eyes shut. 'And five, six, seven, eight . . .' He jumped in the air, pointed his toes . . . and stopped.

'Is that it?' asked Jeffrey.

Zack gave a light laugh. 'Of course not!

Hold on, I'll start again. And five, six, seven, eight . . . no. No, that's not right. I had it this afternoon. Stop looking at me, I need to think. Five, six, seven, eight . . . no . . . no . . . AAAAAGH!'

'I don't know if punching the wall is going to help,' said Jeffrey.

'I CAN'T DO IT!' howled Zack.

'Calm down,' said Jeffrey. 'You can do it in rehearsals, can't you?'

Zack nodded.

'And you can do it on your own?'

Zack nodded again.

'So it's just having an audience that's making

78

it difficult,' pondered Jeffrey. 'Well, you know what they say: "It'll be all right on the night!"'

'But supposing it isn't?' said Zack.

Jeffrey pushed his glasses up his nose. 'I think you need to talk to someone about this,' he said. 'Maybe . . . your director?'

'No,' said Zack. 'It's too embarrassing.'

'All right, not your director,' said Jeffrey. 'But this is just nerves, after all. Everyone gets them from time to time. I don't, of course, but I'm not an actor. Oh, I know! You should talk to Ellie May! She's very experienced – I'm sure she'll be able to help you.'

Zack's mouth dropped open. 'No no no!' he squeaked. 'Not Ellie May!'

'I know she's very famous and everything,' said Jeffrey, 'but you really mustn't be scared of her. She's ever so nice.'

'Don't you dare tell Ellie May,' spluttered Zack. 'You've got to promise you won't. You've got to.'

'Well . . .' said Jeffrey.

'*Promise*,' said Zack, his face white with panic.

'All right, I promise I won't tell Ellie May,' said Jeffrey. 'But . . .'

They both heard the lift ping.

Jeffrey got to his feet. 'She's back. Look, Zack, are you sure? Just a quick chat? I bet you'd feel better.'

'No way,' said Zack, his voice as chilly as an igloo.

Jeffrey sighed. 'All right then. Night night, Zack. Nice talking to you. And, at least say you'll think about it?'

'I definitely definitely won't,' said Zack, opening his bedroom door and facing himself in the mirror. 'And five, six, seven, eight . . .'

Chapter Four

Ellie May is Eating a Tiny Hamburger

'Jeffrey,' said Ellie May. 'In your opinion, how many waffles is too many waffles?'

'That would depend,' said Jeffrey, 'on exactly what else you have already had to eat.'

'Well,' said Ellie May. 'So far, I have had one slice of toast with raspberry jam on it. I have had four pancakes, two with maple syrup on them and two with just sugar, and half a melon cut up into little pieces. I have had some eggs over easy, to find out what they are, and also some eggs sunny side up, and it turns out that they are both types of fried egg. So I have had a lot of fried eggs. Also, I had a bit of bacon and a sausage. And a croissant. A piece of sushi because it was there even though I didn't really want it but actually it was quite yummy although to be honest I probably won't have it for breakfast again. And a glass of orange juice and then another glass of orange juice. And some fudge cake. Plus I took some grapefruit but it was a bit sour so I didn't eat it.'

'Well,' said Jeffrey, pausing to take a delicate sip of his tea, 'in that case, I would say that even one waffle would be too many waffles.'

'Hmm,' said Ellie May. 'Yes. I see your point. Excuse me, Jeffrey. I just have to go and speak to someone.' She got to her feet and set off after the nearest waitress. 'Sorry about this, but I have an urgent message for the chef. It's about my order. The one that was mainly waffles . . .'

Jeffrey finished his raspberry yogurt with real raspberries in it, and looked around. The breakfast room of The Hotel Splendido Marvellousa was a splendid and marvellous place. A brass band was playing 'Morning Has Broken' in one corner, while, overhead, hummingbirds swooped and dived through an actual rainbow, which had been created using running water, bright lights and an awful lot of money.

And, hiding behind a palm tree covered in real monkeys, Jeffrey caught a flash of bright blond hair. It was a lean, wiry boy, moving carefully and precisely on his strong, pointed toes. A boy walking very slowly and deliberately so that he could move unseen across the breakfast room. A boy who definitely didn't want to make eye contact with Jeffrey. A boy who –

'Morning, Zack!' called Jeffrey.

'How are you feeling today? Any better?'

Zack looked around. 'Were you talking to me?' he asked.

'Yes,' said Jeffrey. 'Who else would I be talking to? One of the monkeys, I suppose, but . . . well, look,

anyway, I've been a bit worried about you.'

'I'm all right, thank you,' said Zack.

'I mean, I had a terrible dream last night

where I was on stage and the curtain

came up and I just froze, in front of

everyone, and the audience was booing. And then the theatre started filling with spiders and rats. But, you know, other than that it's fine.'

'No, it isn't,' said Jeffrey. 'It's not fine. And . . . hello, Ellie May.'

'She's going to see if she can cancel my order,' said Ellie May, plunking back down into her seat.

'Good,' said Jeffrey. 'I was just talking to Za– Oh. He's gone.'

'Look at this,' said Ellie May, holding out a thick white envelope. 'The waitress gave it to me just now.' She tore it open.

To celebrate our splendidly marvellous celebrity guests

THE HOTEL SPLENDIDO MARVELLOUSA

invites you to

a splendidly marvellous brunch

in

❧ The Grand Ballroom ☙

11 a.m.

Don't be late!

(A little bit late is fine.)

'Brunch!' squeaked Ellie May. 'I love brunch! I love it so much! What is brunch, exactly? I mean, I do basically know, but –'

Jeffrey put down his teacup. 'It's a cross between breakfast and lunch,' he said. 'I got an invitation too. I think everyone in the hotel did.'

'Oh,' said Ellie May, remembering Zack's triumphant grin. Would he be at the brunch, showing off his dancing and laughing at her rubbishy Top Q? Of course he would. 'Maybe I'll leave it . . .'

Jeffrey frowned. 'Really? That's not like you.'

'No,' said Ellie May. 'I suppose not.' She

looked around the dining room, trying to decide what to do.

'You look terribly serious,' said Jeffrey. 'Oh, I know what will cheer you up. Did you see that they have real monkeys in that fake tree?'

'Seriously?' said Ellie May. 'Oooh, yes, there they are! Will you take my photo with them? Use my phone. Quick!'

Ellie May ran to the tree and grinned at Jeffrey.

'Right, stay still,' he said. 'Can you try to move just a bit to your right? No, that's my right, no, hold on, the monkeys keep moving, oh dear, I think one's just jumped on my head.'

He handed
Ellie May her
phone. 'How's this?'
he asked. 'I took a few.'

Ellie May tapped
at the screen, and there,
suddenly, was the picture
of her with Katsu and Kiko.

Ellie May smiled.

It didn't matter at all that she couldn't sing
and dance and act. Even Kiko couldn't do all three

and she was the most amazing person on the planet.

'Can we go and sit back down again?' asked Jeffrey. 'Because I'm getting a bit covered with monkeys.'

'Do you know, I think I *will* go to the brunch after all,' said Ellie May, making her way back over to their table. 'And that means we can go shopping for a brunch outfit, doesn't it, Jeffrey?'

'Or we could prepare for your TV interview,' said Jeffrey, shaking a monkey from his elbow. Ellie May stared at him. 'You know, think of a few exciting stories to tell about your film, that kind of thing.'

93

'*Or*, we could go shopping,' said Ellie May.

Jeffrey wiped a bit of monkey poo from his shoulder. When he looked up, Ellie May was waiting expectantly. 'All right,' he said. 'Shopping it is.'

'Hooray!' cried Ellie May, leaping up and almost crashing into a waitress.

'Hi there,' said the waitress. 'Can you move that teapot out of the way for me, please? Someone at this table ordered twenty-seven waffles.'

A short while later, Ellie May stood in the ballroom of The Hotel Splendido Marvellousa with Jeffrey at her side. It was a marvellously splendid brunch, filled with splendidly marvellous people. Ellie May's T-shirt was splendid, and her hat was marvellous. And best of all, she was feeling as marvellously splendid as she looked.

'Oh, Kiko's not here,' said Jeffrey sadly. 'I was hoping she'd sign my book. But there's Chuck Palaver.' He pointed at a man with a tanned, round face, which reminded Ellie May very slightly of a pumpkin. 'You're doing his TV show tomorrow night.'

'Amazing!' cried Ellie May. 'I'm going to say hello.'

She pranced across the room and grabbed Chuck Palaver by his orange hand.

'I'm Ellie May,' said Ellie May.

'Chuck Palaver,' said Chuck Palaver. 'Say, I'm interviewing you, aren't I? For my starlet special.'

'That's right,' beamed Ellie May. 'Now, would you like me to have any exciting stories ready? To make it more exciting? I should have thought of some already but I had to go shopping for a brunch outfit. Sorry.'

'I'm sure you're plenty exciting just as you

are,' said Chuck Palaver.

'Well, let me know if you change your mind,' said Ellie May. 'Because I have a very lively imagination, and –'

She felt someone tap her on the shoulder.

'Word, Ellie May,' said Zack.

'Ellie May is two words,' said Ellie May.

'No, "word" means hello,' said Zack.

'No, "*hello*" means hello,' said Ellie May. 'Anyway, hello, Zack. I'm afraid I'm a bit busy at the moment, so if you could just come back later and . . .'

'Hey there, Mr Palaver,' said Zack. 'I'm

Zack-short-for-Zachary-but-everyone-calls-me-Zack and I'm in a Broadway show!'

'And you probably have to go to a rehearsal or something, I should think,' said Ellie May. 'Bye bye.'

'I don't have a rehearsal until this afternoon,' said Zack.

'And what do you do in this Broadway show?' asked Chuck Palaver.

'Lots of different things,' said Zack. 'Acting, singing, dancing, saying lines, there's a bit where I have to climb a ladder . . .' He glanced at Ellie May. 'Basically, I'm really talented, which is important when you're a proper actor.'

'It sure is,' said Chuck Palaver. 'And what's your favourite? Singing, dancing or acting?'

'That's a difficult one,' said Zack. 'But if I really had to choose, I'd say . . . all three.'

Meanwhile, Jeffrey found himself next to Kiko's spokesman, who was thoughtfully eating a very small sandwich.

'Hi again,' said Jeffrey. 'How's everything going?'

'Kiko has no statement to make at this time,' said Kiko's spokesman.

'Really?' said Jeffrey. 'Ellie May has lots of statements to make at this time.'

'Oh, so you're a spokesman now, are you?' said Kiko's spokesman.

'Yes,' said Jeffrey. 'I am. And I'd like to state for the record that Ellie May is very much enjoying her stay. Ellie May thinks that The Hotel Splendido Marvellousa is fantastic. Ellie May is eating fudge cake.'

'Is she?' asked Kiko's spokesman.

'I can't see her right now,' said Jeffrey,

standing on his tiptoes and peering around the room, 'but she usually is at about this time. And most times.'

Kiko's spokesman tried not to smile.

'There she is,' said Jeffrey. 'Ellie May isn't eating fudge cake. She's eating a sausage on a stick. Now she's eating a tiny hamburger. And now she's eating fudge cake. How am I doing?'

'You're a natural,' laughed Kiko's spokesman. 'I think you could definitely be a spokesman if you wanted.'

'Oooh!' grinned Jeffrey. 'A natural!'

Kiko's spokesman finished his sandwich. 'Let

me test you. How does Ellie May feel about . . . New York?'

'Ellie May is having a wonderful time in New York and looks forward to returning here in the future,' said Jeffrey.

'How's Ellie May's new film going?' said Kiko's spokesman.

'Ellie May is really excited about her new film and can't wait for her fans to see it,' said Jeffrey.

'And is Ellie May enjoying herself this morning?' asked Kiko's spokesman.

'Yes, Ellie May is enjoying herself very much indeed,' said Jeffrey, glancing over to check.

'Except, that's not how she looks when she's enjoying herself. Oh dear. No, she's not enjoying herself at all. Will you excuse me? I think I'd better see if she's all right.'

'So I think my main ambition is to have an internationally successful album and maybe do some stadium tours, but also to win an Oscar and have someone create a ballet just for me,' continued Zack. 'Not forgetting the theatre, of course, which is my first love. Did I tell you that I'm in a Broadway show opening this weekend on Broadway?'

'Films are the best,' said Ellie May. 'I love being in films.'

'But they're just one form of entertainment, aren't they,' said Zack. 'I'd hate it if that was all I could do. I don't want to limit myself.'

'I'm sure you'll go far,' nodded Chuck Palaver.

'And me!' said Ellie May. 'I'm sure I'll go far too. Even further than I've already gone, which is really really far. Because I've got loads of amazingly amazing ambitions. Far more amazing than Zack's. Like . . . for example . . .'

'An album?' supplied Chuck Palaver.

'Maybe,' said Ellie May. Then she remembered her Top Q. 'Well, probably not, actually. Not everyone has to be able to do everything, you know.'

'Yes, they do,' said Zack. 'All the best people are multi-talented. Like me. And Kiko!'

'Ah, Kiko,' said Chuck Palaver. 'If only I could get her on my show. She's a sensation.'

'Exactly,' said Zack.

And as Zack preened and grinned, and flicked his hair and pointed his toes, Ellie May felt the secret begin to stir deep inside her. It started as a tiny little pip, but she could feel it growing larger and more impatient, as though it wanted nothing more than to be set free.

She clenched her jaw and tried to think of something else.

'She acts, she sings, she dances . . . and have you read her books?' marvelled Chuck Palaver. 'It's hard to believe there's so much talent in just one person.'

Ellie May shut her eyes as the secret pulsed and swelled. It snaked down her arms and pressed against her chest, and for a terrible moment, she thought she might burst.

'I basically see Kiko as my role model,' said Zack, smiling in a way that somehow made Ellie May want to scream. 'And . . . well, it's a bit hush-hush really . . . let's change the subject.'

'Let's,' gasped Ellie May. 'Let's change the subject and never talk about Kiko again.'

'OK,' said Chuck Palaver.

'OK,' said Ellie May, swallowing hard. 'So, Chuck, what do you think I should wear for the interview, then? Because I don't have my full wardrobe with me, but I'm sure that –'

'All right, I wasn't going to say anything, but you forced it out of me,' said Zack. 'Kiko's not just my role model. She's my friend, too.'

And now the secret was spreading to the very tips of Ellie May's fingers and up her neck and into her mouth . . .

'I met her this morning by the spa,' continued Zack, 'and we were talking about maybe heading into the studio together to lay down some tracks. Nothing's confirmed yet, of course, but it's pretty awesome.'

'No, you didn't,' said Ellie May.

'Yes, I did,' said Zack. 'It's really sad that you can't sing, Ellie May, and it's a shame that you're not friends with Kiko, but there's no need to accuse me of lying.'

'I mean,' said Ellie May giddily, 'you didn't meet Kiko. If you talked about going into the studio to record music then it must have been her identical twin sister, Katsu. Oh, didn't you know that Kiko doesn't do her own singing and dancing? She gets Katsu to do it. Maybe you're not such good friends with her after all.'

Zack's mouth dropped open. 'What?'

'What?' said Chuck Palaver.

'*What?*' said Jeffrey.

The room had gone very, very quiet.

'Um, nothing!' said Ellie May, feeling a nasty

heat prickle at her cheeks. 'Forget I said anything. I didn't say anything. I'm not even here.'

'Kiko has a secret identical twin sister?' cried Chuck Palaver.

'Kiko doesn't do her own singing and dancing?' cried Zack.

'Kiko has no statement to make at this time,' said Kiko's spokesman stiffly, his eyes darting left and right.

'And nor does Ellie May,' cried Jeffrey, as everyone in the ballroom started to move in towards their little group. He caught Ellie May by the arm and steered her over to the door.

'I didn't want to tell . . .' began Ellie May. 'I mean, I did, but I –'

'Please don't say anything else!' hissed Jeffrey. 'Not one word!'

They reached the lobby and glanced back to see that Kiko's spokesman had almost disappeared beneath the crowd.

'No!' he called, as he vanished into a swarm of people. 'Please! Everyone, get back! Let me go. Kiko has no statement to make at this time. Kiko has no statement to make at this time! Aaaaaaaargh!'

Chapter Five

Ellie May Will be Fine as Long as she Doesn't Move Very Much

Ellie May lay in her king-sized bed, feeling extremely comfortable and sleepy. She'd just had a lovely dream about something to do with a kitten, and now the sun shone down upon her snuggly duvet and soft, soft pillows. Yes, it was going to be another really good day.

Except . . . except . . . as Ellie May's eyelids flickered and she wiggled her toes against those crisp cotton sheets, somewhere, somehow, she knew that something was a tiny little bit wrong. No, not a tiny little bit wrong. Whatever it was, it was very wrong indeed.

But what was it?

She didn't feel ill.

She hadn't somehow turned blue.

So maybe everything was fine after all.

'Morning, Ellie May.'

Ellie May sat up in bed as Jeffrey opened the

door. He gave her a small, unhappy smile. The sort of smile that's really a frown in fancy dress.

And then Ellie May remembered what she'd done.

But perhaps, if she tried really hard, she could unremember it again. At least for a little while.

'Good morning, Jeffrey,' said Ellie May. 'What shall we do today? Maybe a bit of sightseeing, before my big interview tonight? I don't know if there's much to see in New York, but I'm sure we'll find something. Maybe a museum. You like museums . . .' she tailed off.

'Well, the problem is that we may not be able

to get out of the hotel very easily,' said Jeffrey. 'Look.' He pointed to the window and Ellie May looked down. The whole street was full of reporters. Reporters holding cameras and notebooks and telescopes and standing on cars and climbing up lamp posts. They stretched for as far as she could see, milling and pushing towards the hotel doors like a sea that was not made of water but instead had been created from a huge crowd of people who all wanted to look at Kiko.

'Wow,' said Ellie May, with a brightness she didn't quite feel. 'Oh, and there's a helicopter. Two helicopters.' She flicked on the TV.

'. . . and the question we're all asking: Does Kiko really have an identical twin sister? Is it possible to keep something like that a secret for so long? Joining me today on my expert panel, we have . . .'

Ellie May changed the channel.

'. . . and today the eyes of the world are on

The Hotel Splendido Marvellousa in New York, where it's rumoured that Kiko is staying with her secret identical twin sister! We'll be bringing you the latest from right outside the lobby . . .'

Ellie May changed the channel.

'These naughty puppies are *double trouble*!'

Ellie May changed the channel.

'They're cookies, yes, but with a *secret* ingredient . . .'

Ellie May turned the television off.

Maybe she couldn't unremember it after all.

'They trusted you,' said Jeffrey.

'I know,' whispered Ellie May.

'When someone tells you a secret, you keep it,' said Jeffrey.

'I *know*,' said Ellie May, her mouth starting to wobble.

'So, if you know, then why did you tell?' asked Jeffrey.

'I'm not sure,' said Ellie May. Jeffrey waited. 'Well, maybe I am,' she admitted. 'I was showing off to Zack.'

'But why?' asked Jeffrey.

Ellie May slithered down under her duvet. 'Because he's so good at everything all the time and I felt rubbish because I can't sing and I tried doing the splits yesterday and I thought I was going to snap.'

'But that doesn't matter,' said Jeffrey, 'because you're brilliant at being a film star.'

'Zack said it mattered,' moaned Ellie May. 'I wish I was like him. He's amazing.'

Jeffrey looked down at Ellie May, so small and miserable, and remembered Zack's white, frightened face as he'd struggled with his dance routine.

'I'm sure Zack isn't as confident as he seems,' said Jeffrey.

'I'm sure he is,' said Ellie May.

Jeffrey opened his mouth . . . and remembered his promise to Zack . . . and closed it again.

'Well, anyway,' he said, 'what are we going to do now? Did you want to go to a museum? Or would you like to go and tell Kiko and Katsu that you're sorry?'

'Neither,' said Ellie May. 'I want to go back to bed. Maybe if I can sleep for long enough everyone will forget all about this.' She glanced back out of the window. The reporters were still there. She'd probably have to go to sleep for an incredibly long time. But Sleeping Beauty had slept for a hundred years, so maybe . . .

'Ellie May,' prompted Jeffrey.

'Did *you* want to go to a museum?' asked Ellie May hopefully.

Jeffrey shook his head.

Ellie May got to her feet. 'All right then,' she said. 'Let's go.'

'Er, hello?' called Ellie May. 'Kiko? Are you there? Kiko! Katsu? It's me! Ellie May! That's just in case you didn't recognise my voice!'

The door opened.

'Ellie May,' said Kiko's spokesman. He said it carefully, and slowly, as though the words tasted horrible.

'Yes, that's right,' smiled Ellie May. 'Can I come in, please? I have something very important I need to say.'

'No,' said Kiko's spokesman.

'Are you sure?' asked Ellie May. 'I could maybe just come in for a little bit?'

'No,' said Kiko's spokesman.

'How about if I went in and out really really fast?' asked Ellie May. 'So fast that you didn't even notice I'd done it?'

'No,' said Kiko's spokesman.

'Well, maybe Kiko left a message for me?' asked Ellie May.

'Kiko has no statement to make at this time,' said Kiko's spokesman.

'She must have said *something*,' said Ellie May. 'Even if it was an angry something. Don't worry, I can take it. I hope.'

'Kiko has no statement to make at this time,' said Kiko's spokesman.

Jeffrey took Ellie May's arm. 'Let's just leave it,' he whispered.

Kiko's spokesman stood to one side as a

waiter stepped past him with an enormous tray of tropical fruit.

'OK,' said Ellie May. 'Thank you anyway, Mr Spokesman.'

They watched the door slam shut.

Ellie May smiled. 'Are you thinking what I'm thinking?' she asked.

Jeffrey studied Ellie May's mischievous face. 'Probably not,' he admitted.

'Let's go back upstairs,' said Ellie May. 'Because I've just had an amazingly amazing idea . . .'

Ellie May and Jeffrey stood in the hotel corridor in their smart new uniforms. Ellie May's hair was tucked under a long black wig, while Jeffrey had sprayed his curls grey. And their faces were almost unrecognisable. Ellie May had spent an awfully long time in costume trailers and she knew a thing or two about using make-up as a disguise. In fact, she knew seven things, and they all involved eyeliner.

'I'm really not sure about this,' said Jeffrey.

'Then it's a good thing that I am,' said Ellie May. 'Now, are you ready to do some acting?'

'I suppose so,' sighed Jeffrey. 'How are you doing in those shoes?'

Ellie May's trousers were far too long for her, so she was wearing the highest pair of high heels she had. And she'd strapped them on to some plastic cups, to make them even higher.

'I will be fine as long as I don't move very much,' said Ellie May. 'Give me a push, Jeffrey? OK, let's go.'

Kiko's spokesman watched from the door of Kiko's suite as the bizarre pair tottered round the corner.

'Hello,' said Jeffrey, in his deepest voice. 'We're here to change Kiko's sheets.'

'We work for the hotel,' said Ellie May.

'As sheet changers.'

Kiko's spokesman pursed his lips. 'You look a bit . . .'

'Familiar?' growled Jeffrey. 'Because we're not. We've never seen you before in our lives.'

'No, not familiar,' said Kiko's spokesman. 'Odd. What happened to your face?'

'I had an accident a very long time ago. I don't ever talk about it. Too upsetting. Can we come in?' said Jeffrey.

'I suppose so,' said Kiko's spokesman.

'Hooray!' cried Ellie May.

'Except,' said Kiko's spokesman, 'where are

your sheets? If you're here to change the sheets, shouldn't you have some sheets?'

'Ellie May's supposed to have the sheets,' said Jeffrey. 'I mean . . . oops.'

Kiko's spokesman moved to block the door. '*Is she?*'

'Oh, no!' cried Ellie May. And then, 'I think I'm going to fall over. Can someone catch me, please?'

'Right,' said Ellie May. 'The problem last time was my shoes and forgetting the sheets and also the bit where you called me Ellie May. But those things shouldn't matter this time.'

'I suppose not,' said Jeffrey, who was now wearing Ellie May's black wig over his hair and pushing a room-service trolley. He caught a glimpse of his reflection in a silver coffee pot. 'Oh dear, I look ever so silly.'

'You look absolutely fantastic,' said Ellie May. 'Even better than usual. Can you do a different voice this time?'

'If you insist,' said Jeffrey. 'And you're sure that taking off my glasses is enough of a disguise?'

'Yes,' said Ellie May. 'You look completely different. Although I can do some more make-up on you if you like –'

'No thank you,' said Jeffrey swiftly, putting his glasses into his pocket. 'Right, in you get.'

Ellie May climbed inside the trolley and Jeffrey adjusted its white tablecloth until she was completely covered.

'Off we go,' said Jeffrey. 'Hold on, what's that munching noise?'

'I found some crisps,' said Ellie May.

Jeffrey crossed his fingers as they came round the corner.

'Room service for Kiko,' he squeaked.

'I don't think Kiko ordered anything,' said Kiko's spokesman.

'She must have done, or I wouldn't be here,' piped Jeffrey. 'I've got all sorts of delicious yummy things that she'll definitely want to eat. Like . . . erm . . . crisps . . . and . . . anyway, let me in please or they'll get cold. Because they're . . . special . . . hot . . . crisps.'

Kiko's spokesman stepped back. 'All right,' he said. 'Hey, where are you going?'

'I'm not totally sure,' said Jeffrey. 'My eyesight's a bit . . . hold on, this way . . .'

'Those are the stairs,' said Kiko's spokesman.

'Are they?' said Jeffrey.

'Yes!' cried Kiko's spokesman. 'Stop . . . I said, *stop . . .*'

'Waaaaaaaaaaaaaaaaaaaaaaaaaaaaaa!' shrieked Ellie May, as the room-service trolley hurtled down the steps, throwing her out on to the carpet. 'AaaaaaaaaaaaaaaaaaaaaaaaaaaaaarRUMPH!' she yelled, as the trolley, and then Jeffrey, landed on top of her, followed by a light sprinkling of crisps.

Jeffrey sat up and rubbed his nose. 'Oh dear. Are you all right, Ellie May?'

Ellie May groaned and shook crisp crumbs

134

from her hair. 'You're not supposed to call me Ellie May.'

'Sorry, I mean, what did we say your code name was? Oh, yes, it was Emily! Are you all right, *Emily*?'

Ellie May looked up to see Kiko's spokesman folding his arms. 'Yes, thank you, *Godfrey*. But maybe we should go and deliver this lovely food to someone else.'

The plant stood in the silent corridor of

The Hotel Splendido Marvellousa. It was a beautiful plant, with glossy green leaves and big yellow flowers and a spotted bow tie. Next to it stood a large suitcase. A large suitcase with bright-pink toenails.

Plant spoke first. 'So,' it said, in its worried voice, 'we just get as close to the door as we can and then wait?'

'Till he leaves,' said Suitcase. 'Then we go inside.'

'All right,' said Plant.

They sidled round the corner and up next to the door. And then they waited.

And waited.

And waited.

And waited.

And waited.

And waited.

'I need the loo,' said Suitcase.

'Can you hold on?' asked Plant.

'I'll try,' said Suitcase.

They waited a bit more.

The door opened, and out came Kiko's spokesman, wearing his coat and carrying an umbrella.

'Bye,' he called. Then he stopped. 'Huh. That plant wasn't there this morning.'

'Yes it was,' said Plant.

'And how come there's a suitcase here? Is it one of ours?' He turned and shouted back into the room, 'Are we missing a case? No, I thought not. Must be a mistake. I'll take it back to the lobby.' He went to lift it up and . . . 'Ouch, my poor back! What on earth is in here? Bricks? Lead? Oh my gosh, it's *moving* . . .' He unzipped the case. 'Ah.'

'Hi there,' said Ellie May. 'Sorry about your back. Would you like me to fetch you some ice? I'll get it just as soon as I've had a quick word with Kiko and Katsu.'

Kiko's spokesman stood very still, while his face went from normal-coloured to pink, to red, to a deep and furious purple.

'No,' he said. 'You are not going in there. Do you understand me? Not today, not tomorrow, not ever.'

From inside her suitcase, Ellie May nodded.

'I suppose you think this is all very funny,' said Kiko's spokesman. 'Well, it isn't. Years of hard work, of being careful, of hiding and disguising, and you've ruined the whole lot. Even if I could let you in, I wouldn't. Kiko's completely heartbroken. Heartbroken! And what's Katsu supposed to do? What are either of them supposed to do now? You've caused enough damage, Ellie May. Leave us alone.'

Ellie May clambered out of the suitcase and got to her feet.

'I don't think it's funny,' she said. 'I feel terrible. Properly awful.'

'Then you're experiencing just a tiny bit of what poor Kiko is feeling,' said Kiko's spokesman. 'Now, go away and don't ever come back.'

'OK,' whispered Ellie May, as the door slammed in her face.

'Please don't be sad,' said Jeffrey desperately, pulling a bit of plant from behind his ear. 'I bet the reason they don't want to see you is that they've forgiven you already.'

'I'm sure they haven't,' wept Ellie May. 'Why would they? I wouldn't if it were me. I mean, if they were me. And I were . . . them.'

She found her phone and gazed once more at the picture, which rippled and shook through a film of tears. Kiko and Katsu looked back at her from the screen, Katsu smiling cheerfully, Kiko flinching from the camera flash. 'I can't make it OK again, can I?' sobbed Ellie May. 'I'll just have to be sad and sorry forever and ever and ever.'

'You must stop crying,' said Jeffrey, dabbing at Ellie May's flushed cheeks with a hanky that smelled of lavender. 'You're going on TV soon, and you can't do your interview like this.'

Ellie May sniffed. 'My interview. I'd forgotten about that.'

'Even though it's the whole reason we're here in the first place,' sighed Jeffrey, holding the handkerchief over Ellie May's pink nose. 'Blow, please.'

Ellie May blew.

And then she had an idea. A very good idea. An even better idea than the pretending-to-be-a-suitcase idea.

Well, maybe not *better* than that, but definitely at least as good.

Chapter Six

Ellie May is Really Really Really Sorry

'Wow, Jeffrey, look at that,' sighed Ellie May.

'What?' asked Jeffrey.

'New York,' said Ellie May. 'There! Out the window!'

'I see it,' said Jeffrey.

'There's the Empire Cake Building,' said Ellie May.

'The Empire *State* Building,' said Jeffrey.

'And there's another big building that's also famous, probably,' said Ellie May, 'and there's a hotdog stand and there's another hotdog stand and there's a tree!'

'And here's the TV studio,' said Jeffrey, opening the limousine door.

'Hi there!'

A swishy-haired lady with a clipboard was grinning down into the car.

'Welcome to *The Chuck Palaver Show*! We're

all so excited about having you here tonight can you please tell me your name thank you great.'

'It's Ellie May,' said Ellie May.

'That's great. Would you like to follow me to hair and make-up and then you can meet Chuck himself he's so great.'

'Great,' said Ellie May.

'Great,' said Jeffrey.

'Great,' said the lady. 'Right, here we are. The studio is just down there and we'll be live very soon. If you'd like to go and see make-up and then I'll come and get you and we'll head down to Chuck Palaver's sofa great.'

The New York day had turned into a New York night. One wall of Chuck Palaver's studio was made of glass, and as Ellie May stepped round the television cameras she could see the city lit up like a Christmas tree in the shape of New York.

Ellie May held out her phone to take a photo.

'Turn that off great,' said the swishy-haired lady, guiding Ellie May across the set towards Chuck Palaver's famous sofa, upon which sat Cassie Craven and . . .

'Pssst, Ellie May,' said Zack.

'Live in thirty seconds,' said the lady, backing away through the TV cameras. 'Good luck! You're going to be just great.'

'Chuck Palaver interviewed me about being a star on Broadway,' whispered Zack as Ellie May climbed on to the sofa. 'Isn't that awesome?'

'Five seconds. Four. Three . . .'

Chuck Palaver swung around and addressed

the nearest camera. 'Welcome back, everybody. It's

a Chuck Palaver starlet special this evening. We've

had the inside story on the life of a Broadway baby,

150

Cassie Craven's just been telling us why she won't be doing any more interviews, and now it's over to screen sensation Ellie May. She's got a new movie coming out next week. Ellie May, would you like to tell us a bit about it?'

Ellie May felt the TV lights warm her cheeks. 'Thanks, Chuck. Yes, I'm really excited about my new film. It's called *Oranges and Lemons*. I play a girl who lives on a lemon farm in olden times. Everything is very sad until I invent lemonade and then we get rich and then I invent orange squash and then it's the end.'

'Oh, really?' said Chuck Palaver.

'Yes,' Ellie May went on. 'Luckily, I quite like citrus fruit. Anyway, it was a lot of fun to make and I hope people enjoy it.'

'Fantastic,' said Chuck Palaver. He turned to the camera. 'So, there we have it. Ellie May, everyone. Now, to the results of our competition . . .'

'Wait,' cried Ellie May. 'There's something else.'

This was it.

Any moment now and everything would be all right again.

Well, maybe not all right, but at least it would be a bit less wrong.

Ellie May smiled a nervous smile. 'There's

something I need to say. It's about Kiko.'

Chuck Palaver sat up. 'What about her?'

Ellie May shifted on the sofa. 'You've probably all seen a lot of stuff recently about Kiko and her identical twin sister, Katsu,' she said. 'Well, it was my fault.'

'And can you tell our viewers why?' asked Chuck Palaver.

'We're all staying at the same hotel,' said Ellie May. 'I met them, and they asked me to keep their secret, but I didn't. I told everyone. So,' she looked straight into the camera, hoping that the twins were watching, 'I want them to know that I'm sorry.

Really really really sorry. I'd do anything to make it OK again and I feel awful.'

Chuck Palaver nodded. 'Yes, America, I was there when she said it.' He turned back to Ellie May. 'So, just to be completely clear, Kiko has an identical twin who sings and dances for her?'

Ellie May nodded an unhappy nod.

'And while we've been thinking that Kiko is the most talented woman on earth, half the time we've been watching her sister?'

'I know,' said Ellie May. 'I almost can't believe they managed to keep it a secret for so long.'

'Me neither,' said Chuck Palaver. 'In fact, I

can't believe it at all.'

The studio lights burned as Chuck Palaver leaned forwards.

'You're a clever girl, Ellie May, so I think you'll agree, it doesn't seem very likely, does it? How come we haven't seen her?'

'She wears a pink wig,' said Ellie May helpfully. 'And sometimes a fat suit.'

'Maybe she does,' said Chuck Palaver. 'Or maybe she doesn't exist.'

'She does!' cried Ellie May.

'Perhaps . . .' said Chuck Palaver. 'But, to be honest, I don't think Kiko's staying in your hotel.

It's been surrounded for days and no one's caught so much as a glimpse of her. She wasn't at the brunch. And, just before you came on, Cassie was telling me that she'd heard Kiko was staying in London.'

Cassie Craven giggled and fluffed up her hair.

'Don't worry, Ellie May,' said Chuck Palaver. 'You can tell us the truth. I used to make up stories when I was young. Everyone does. It's nothing to be ashamed of.'

'I don't make things up,' said Ellie May.

'Sure you do,' said Chuck Palaver. 'You were the one who told me that you have a lively imagination. And imagination is making things up. Right?'

'But it's *true*,' insisted Ellie May. 'You have to trust me. Kiko *does* have a sister. I've met her. In fact, I've got proof!'

'What kind of proof?' asked Chuck Palaver.

'There's a ph-photo,' stammered Ellie May, 'of the three of us all together.' She pulled her phone from her pocket and turned it on.

Chuck Palaver rubbed his hands. 'If you're just joining us then this is *The Chuck Palaver Show* and, after huge speculation, we're about to see final, definite evidence that Kiko really does have a secret identical twin sister. Yes, we have the first ever picture of the two of them together. Live! Exclusive! Ellie May, if you could please show the cameras . . .'

Ellie May looked down into her lap. Katsu and Kiko looked back up at her. Trusting her to keep their secret.

'Sorry,' she whispered.

'Ellie May?' prompted Chuck Palaver. 'The whole world is waiting . . .'

Kiko's eyes met hers.

And then, suddenly, painfully, Ellie May knew exactly what she had to do.

'So, here we are, the first ever picture of Kiko

and her secret twin – wait a minute, that's not Kiko.'

Downstairs in the dressing room, Jeffrey watched along with millions of others as the television camera zoomed in on a photo of Ellie May in the dining room of The Hotel Splendido Marvellousa, between two grinning monkeys.

'There we have it,' said Chuck Palaver. 'And it's just as I thought. There never was a secret identical twin. See you after the break!'

Chapter Seven

Ellie May Must be Happy All Day and All Night

'Ellie May, look! It's Times Square! Aren't the lights wonderful!' said Jeffrey, as the limousine sped beneath an enormous advert for a new kind of chocolate that helped you lose weight.

'And there's the Vampire State Building,' said Ellie May.

'The *Empire* State Build– oh, never mind,' said Jeffrey. 'Anyway. That was a really good thing you did just now. I know Katsu and Kiko will be so grateful.'

Ellie May rubbed her eyes. 'I hope so,' she said wearily. 'You don't suppose that everyone else will be like Chuck Palaver, do you?'

'Goodness me, no,' said Jeffrey. 'I'll be surprised if anyone else even mentions it.'

'Phew,' said Ellie May, as the limo drew up outside the hotel. 'Because, to be honest, if even one more person asks me about Kiko this evening I think I might explode. Or cry. Or do both at the same time, which would be amazing but also quite bad.'

Jeffrey gave Ellie May his most reassuring grin as he opened the car door. 'Look,' he said. 'You're always telling me that I worry too much. Well, now I'm telling you not to worry. It's going to be absolutely fi–'

'THERE SHE IS!'

'ELLIE MAY, WHAT MADE YOU START INVENTING STORIES ABOUT KIKO?'

'DID YOU DO IT FOR THE ATTENTION, ELLIE MAY?'

'DO YOU NEED PUBLICITY, ELLIE MAY?'

'ELLIE MAY, WILL YOU APOLOGISE TO KIKO?'

It was the same crowd of reporters that had been trying to catch a glimpse of Kiko and Katsu, but now they pushed up around the limo, holding out their cameras and screeching Ellie May's name like a pack of starving hyenas.

'No,' whimpered Ellie May, drawing back into the safety of the car. 'No, you don't understand . . .'

The faces were everywhere, shouting and staring, the camera flashes brighter than lightning. And the hands, holding out microphones, waving, clawing, scratching with their pens . . . and now,

Ellie May understood why Kiko wanted to hide herself away. Now, when it was too late.

'Ellie May, listen to me.'

A familiar voice was calling her name.

'Ellie May, we've got to get out of the car and into the hotel. Take hold of my arm, and put your coat over your head if you want. They'll have to let you through, don't worry. Hold on to my arm and everything will be OK.'

Slowly, as though she were trapped in a horrible, horrible dream, Ellie May took Jeffrey's hand and stepped out into the night.

Then, forwards they pushed, one step, two, three, four, and the crowd yelled and bayed and shrieked until, wonderfully, they were back in the hotel lobby, where it was warm, and safe, and quiet.

Jeffrey caught Ellie May by the shoulders and guided her into a chair.

'Are you OK?' he asked.

When she spoke, Ellie May's voice was unexpectedly calm. 'Yes, thank you,' she said. 'I think I am going to have an early night tonight, Jeffrey. I'll see you tomorrow at breakfast.'

'Are you sure?' asked Jeffrey. 'You've gone awfully pale. We could go to the Energy Zone before bed? Or I'm sure I could get the spa to open up, if you think a pedicure would help?'

'No, thank you,' said Ellie May. Even her own voice sounded far away. 'I'm going to have a lovely lie down and I'll see you in the morning.'

'If you're absolutely certain,' said Jeffrey. 'Night then.'

Ellie May stood in the centre of her sumptuous hotel room. There were nine pillows on her bed, and upon each pillow was balanced a handmade chocolate. And upon each chocolate was balanced another, much smaller handmade chocolate, because that was the way The Hotel Splendido Marvellousa made sure its guests were happy.

But Ellie May wasn't happy.

She didn't want a chocolate, or a pillow. She didn't want a silk dressing gown, or a really quick bath.

She glanced out of the window. Far below, the reporters and photographers were still waiting. In fact, she could almost still hear them shouting at her.

Ellie May pressed a button, and a TV slid

down from the ceiling.

'. . . and the question we're all asking is, can we trust Ellie May? Do any of her stories add up?'

Ellie May changed the channel.

'Does Ellie May actually like fudge cake? Was it even her in all those films?'

Ellie May changed the channel again.

'These naughty puppies are *double* trouble!'

Ellie May sighed so long and so hard that she fell on to her bed, sending chocolates tumbling all over the floor.

Even if everyone thought she was a liar forever and ever, it was worth it to save Kiko's secret. Of course it was. It definitely was. And yes, the entire universe was laughing at her. And OK, now nobody trusted her at all any more. But that was all right. It was the price she had to pay for being so untrustworthy in the first place.

Maybe it would be better if she didn't make new friends from now on. After all, if she'd never met Zack, then right now everything would be perfect. And she didn't exactly *need* friends. She was an incredibly famous film star!

But her hotel room was so big.

And it felt so very, very empty.

Ellie May reached for the phone. 'Hello. Is that

reception? It's Ellie May. I'd like to order a goldfish to be sent to my room, please. In fact, how many have you got? Yes, in that case, I'd like them all. Thank you very much.'

Jeffrey lay on his bed, trying to sleep. It was so late! He was so tired! And Ellie May had looked so strange and so sad.

He slipped out into the corridor and walked towards the lift. Maybe, if he asked very nicely, the restaurant might give him a glass of warm milk.

Jeffrey paused at the splendid sign, with all the marvellous things The Hotel Splendido Marvellousa had to offer, and felt a sudden longing to be somewhere else. A place where the carpets weren't so thick. A place that wasn't covered with cushions. Somewhere . . . normal.

Then he got into the lift and pressed the

button for the roof.

The night air felt wonderful after the perfumed heat of his hotel room. Jeffrey listened to the sirens and cars far below. He'd just stay out for a few minutes and then he'd go back inside.

'Who's there?'

The voice came from the shadows.

'No one,' replied Jeffrey. 'I mean, just me. I was feeling a bit . . . weird . . . all those mirrors . . . you know . . . I didn't realise the roof was occupied.'

'Oh,' said the voice.

Kiko's spokesman stepped into the light.

'Are you all right?' asked Jeffrey.

Kiko's spokesman stared. 'Don't you mean, "Is Kiko all right?"' he said.

'No,' replied Jeffrey. 'I mean you.'

Kiko's spokesman bit his lip, and when he spoke, his voice quivered. 'Sorry,' he said. 'It's just that . . . no one's ever asked about *me* before.'

'Well, I'm asking,' said Jeffrey gently. 'What's the matter?'

'Jeffrey, it's awful,' croaked Kiko's spokesman. 'Kiko and Katsu have been screaming at each other all evening.'

'Because of Ellie May?' asked Jeffrey.

'Yes,' said Kiko's spokesman. 'We were

watching *The Chuck Palaver Show*, and when Ellie May said she'd made everything up, Kiko was so happy. She thought they could go back to how they were. But Katsu's sick of hiding. They keep fighting and fighting and fighting. It's awful! I'll have to go back in there again soon, and I just can't bear it. I *hate* secrets.'

'Me too,' agreed Jeffrey.

'In fact, you know what . . . I don't even like being a spokesman!' cried Kiko's spokesman. 'I've never told anyone this before, but I really wanted to be a nurse.'

'Sometimes I eat Ellie May's fudge cake when

she's not looking,' said Jeffrey. 'I mean, I always replace it before she finds out, but I still feel bad.'

'I hate films,' said Kiko's spokesman. 'Even the ones that Kiko's in. I'd rather watch football.'

'I'm frightened of clowns,' said Jeffrey.

'I can't speak Italian,' said Kiko's spokesman. 'I told Kiko I could when I applied for the job. Now, every time she flies to Rome I have to pretend I've got the flu.'

Jeffrey considered this. 'Well, you know what? I think you can probably come clean on that one. After all, it's not as though you're the first person to have told a white lie to get a job, is it?'

Kiko's spokesman smiled. 'No,' he said. 'I suppose not.' He cleared his throat. 'You know . . . maybe I was a bit harsh on poor Ellie May.'

'She didn't mean to cause so much harm,' said Jeffrey.

'I know she didn't,' said a soft, sad voice.

Jeffrey spun around. 'Hello? Who's that? It's getting awfully crowded up here.'

'It's me,' said Kiko. 'I like to come up here sometimes. To think.'

'And to listen in on other people's private conversations,' said Jeffrey.

'Yes, that too,' admitted Kiko.

'Well, I'm sorry, Kiko,' said Jeffrey, 'but you're not my favourite person right now. I know Ellie May did the wrong thing, but you should have just let her tell you she was sorry. And by the way, I'm really enjoying your new book.'

Kiko sighed. 'I know I'm interrupting,' she said, 'but Katsu just told me she took that photo deliberately. She knew that Ellie May would show everyone. She *wanted* her to show everyone.'

'I see,' said Kiko's spokesman. 'I think.'

'Only, Ellie May didn't show it to anyone,' said Kiko. 'She's better than Katsu thought. She's better than both of us, really.'

'Yes, she is!' said Jeffrey crossly. 'And her reward was being called a liar on national television!'

Kiko gazed out at the lights, far below, and then she nodded. 'You're right,' she said. 'And I'm wrong. I've been wrong for a long time. Now, let me go and see what I can do.'

Ellie May sat in her hotel room. On every shelf there was a bowl, and in every bowl there was a goldfish. There was a goldfish above the fireplace and five goldfish swam in slow circles up on top of her wardrobe. Nine goldfish were balanced around the edge of the bath, and on either side of the bed there was a handy goldfish within arm's reach of the pillow. There were goldfish on the floor and goldfish on the window sill and goldfish on the rug.

'Hmm,' said Ellie May, partly to herself and partly to the goldfish. 'This is one of those ideas that sounds better than it actually is. Like fudge-cake sandwiches. Or maths.'

There was a gentle tap on her bedroom door.

'Hello?' whispered Ellie May.

'Excuse me,' said a small voice. 'I just

wondered if I could borrow a goldfish. Reception said that you had them all.'

Ellie May opened the door. There, looking very pale, and very tired, stood Zack.

'If you want,' said Ellie May. She peered at Zack. 'Shouldn't you be asleep? I thought it was your big day tomorrow.'

'I've just been doing a little bit of last-minute rehearsing,' said Zack. He laughed, lightly, but somehow it didn't sound quite right. 'And I thought maybe I'd sleep better if I had a friend to talk to.'

Ellie May waved at the goldfish bowls. 'Take any one you like,' she said. 'I thought maybe that

having some fish around would make me feel better, but it doesn't seem to be working.'

'But *you* can't feel bad,' said Zack. 'You're an incredibly famous film star. You must be happy all day and all night.'

'And you're going to be in a Broadway show,' said Ellie May. 'So I bet you're amazingly happy.'

They looked at the goldfish, and the goldfish looked back. And then, maybe it was the dark circles beneath Zack's eyes, or maybe it was Ellie May's tear-stained cheeks, but . . .

'I was just saying to the fish that . . . I'm a bit lonely this evening,' said Ellie May. 'I'm not actually very happy right now. I'm not very happy at all.'

Zack looked at the goldfish nearest him, a fat yellow one with bulgy eyes. 'I'm f-frightened about my show tomorrow,' he stuttered. 'I don't think I'll be very good. I don't want to do it any more. I wish I was like you, Ellie May. You're so experienced. You're a proper film star. I don't know what I'm doing and I'll mess it all up and the audience will laugh at me.'

'But Zack,' said Ellie May, 'I get scared before I do a big scene. Everyone does. It's totally normal.'

'Is it?' said Zack. 'No one ever said.'

'Of course,' said Ellie May. 'It's called stage

fright. But it goes away when you start acting. I promise.'

Zack stared. 'Are you sure?'

'I am completely certain,' said Ellie May. 'You'll be fine, Zack. Trust me.'

'I . . . I don't suppose you're free tomorrow evening, are you?' mumbled Zack. 'It might be nice to have a famous film star in the audience.'

Ellie May grinned. 'You won't have a famous film star in the audience, Zack. I mean, you will, but you'll also have a friend. What I mean is that I'm the friend. And the film star. And –'

Someone was calling her name.

'Coming,' said Ellie May. She opened her door, just a crack, to see Kiko's spokesman looking rather hot and dishevelled.

'Have you come to tell me off?' asked Ellie May meekly. 'Because I don't mind if you have, and I know I deserve it, but I just wonder if you could maybe wait until Sunday? When I've gone.'

'Put your TV on,' panted Kiko's spokesman. And then he turned around and dashed back towards the lift.

Zack ran for the TV control, with just one tiny pirouette on the way.

'. . . and you join us live outside The Hotel

Splendido Marvellousa, where we've heard that . . . wait . . . here he is . . .'

The camera swung around to catch Kiko's spokesman racing out through the lobby doors.

'Sorry about that,' he spluttered. 'Right, listen up, everyone. Microphones on? Everyone ready? Good. Because . . . the actress, Kiko, has no statement to make at this time.'

'Oh,' groaned the reporters.

'But . . .' said Kiko's spokesman.

And now the cameras swerved away from the spokesman, to two women standing hand in hand on the hotel steps. One was wearing an old blue sweatshirt, and shielding her face from the cameras.

But no one was looking at her, for all eyes were upon the second woman. Her hair swept long and dark and lovely down her back, and she wore a dress of silvery sequins that shimmered under the lights, as bright and beautiful as all New York.

'But I DO have a statement to make,' she cried. 'I'm here to tell you that I've just started work on a brand new album. It's called *The Secret's Out*. Written and sung by me. Katsu!'

Chapter Eight

Ellie May Probably Doesn't Need to Have Three Televisions

'Hooray!'

'Hooray!'

'Hooray!'

'Hooray!'

The audience rose to its feet and cheered as

the curtain fell on Zack's beaming face.

Ellie May leaned in to Jeffrey. 'Wow,' she said. 'He's really good.'

'Yes,' agreed Jeffrey. 'Eight encores! I'm glad we've stopped clapping, though. Not that he didn't deserve it, but my hands were starting to get a bit sore.'

'And it's still only the interval!' squeaked Ellie May. 'Going to the theatre is brilliant. I think my films should all have intervals in them, too. Look, people are having ice cream, and drinks with straws. Can I have something to drink, Jeffrey? Maybe something fizzy? And do you think they have cake? Or maybe ice cream would be nicer. I know, let's have ice cream *and* cake.'

'I'll see what I can do,' said Jeffrey. He looked down the row of seats. 'Anyone else want anything? Kiko? Katsu? And . . . oh dear, I don't actually know your name. How embarrassing!'

'It's Sebastian,' said Kiko's spokesman, who was really called Sebastian. 'Can I have a chocolate ice cream please? And Kiko would like –'

'I'll have a chocolate ice cream as well,' said Kiko, who was wearing jeans and a grey T-shirt.

'I'll come with you,' said Katsu, who was wearing a scarlet silk dress and, unfortunately for the man sitting behind her, a hat with a great big feather on it. 'You'll need someone to help you carry them.'

'No, no,' said Jeffrey. 'I bet you want to keep a low profile after everything that's happened . . . oh . . .'

Katsu was on her feet, waving like a windmill in a hurricane. 'Hi, everyone, yes, that's right, I'm Katsu. Hi! Hi! Yes, not long until the album's out. Would you like a photo with me? Oh, go on then . . .'

As Katsu and Jeffrey made their slow way across the theatre, Ellie May edged over to Kiko's seat.

Kiko flipped through her programme, which seemed mainly to be black-and-white photos of Zack with his mouth open, and Ellie May tried to decide what, exactly, she would say. She could tell Kiko that it wasn't really her fault. She could maybe try to blame Zack, because if he hadn't been showing off so much then none of this would have happened in the first place.

In fact, she could maybe just talk about the Broadway show and not mention all that secret stuff at all. Actually, that was a really good idea because there was a lot to say about what they'd just seen. In fact, there was one song in particular that Ellie May really wanted to talk about and . . .

Ellie May took a deep, deep breath.

'I'm sorry,' she said.

Kiko looked up from her programme. 'That's all right,' she said.

'Phew,' said Ellie May. 'I was a bit worried. Now, what did you think of Zack's big number, just now –'

'I mean, I suppose I look pretty silly,' continued Kiko, her voice hardening. 'And I had a terrible argument with my sister. And there were nasty articles about me in magazines all around the world. And people were laughing at me on the news. But . . .' She swung round to face Ellie May.

'Yes?' whispered Ellie May.

'I suppose that's my fault, not yours,' said Kiko.

'It's a bit my fault,' said Ellie May.

Kiko shrugged. 'Really, don't worry,' she said. 'Katsu's so happy. And somehow, I feel a lot better too. I used to have dreams that people would find out about us. Terrible, scary dreams. But now they actually have found out, I don't have to worry about it any more! I can just get on with my acting.'

'And writing your novels,' said Ellie May.

'And my novels, yes,' said Kiko. She squinted across the busy theatre. 'Oh dear, Sebastian. I think Katsu might need rescuing.'

Ellie May followed Kiko's gaze to an excited crowd, all waving their cameras.

'She looks like she's having fun,' said Ellie May. 'Come on, let's go over. You can sign some autographs too.'

'I couldn't possibly,' said Kiko, watching her sister posing with a group of fans. 'Or at least . . . I suppose I might sign one, or maybe two . . . but only for tonight.'

'Of course,' said Ellie May.

'Obviously I wouldn't normally,' said Kiko.
'But . . . just this once I could make an exception . . .
Hold on, Katsu, I'm coming!'

Jeffrey returned to find four empty seats.

There were still a few more minutes of the interval left, so he reached down into his bag and pulled out Kiko's novel. Perhaps he could finish it before she came back again. And he could get her to sign it! He opened the book to the final chapter and began to read.

And then, somehow, Jeffrey knew that someone was looking at him. He glanced sideways to see that there, at the very end of the row, sat a slim young woman in sunglasses. A battered notebook lay in her lap, her dark hair was cropped short, and her clothes looked really quite ordinary.

But there was something about the way she was sitting, the shape of her hands, the curve of her shoulder . . . that nagged at Jeffrey.

Where had he seen her before?

As Jeffrey stared, the woman lifted up her sunglasses, just for a moment.

203

Just for a moment, Jeffrey saw the woman's large, dark eyes, and in that same moment he noticed the gold 'K' that hung round her neck . . .

And Jeffrey realised who had really written the book that he held in his hands.

Because it wasn't Kiko.

It wasn't even her twin, Katsu.

It was . . .

The mysterious woman smiled and lifted
her finger to her lips; lips that were exactly the
same as those of her two
identical sisters.

Ellie May
and Jeffrey
looked for the
last time around Ellie May's suite at The Hotel
Splendido Marvellousa. The goldfish were gone,
but the bed was still covered in pillows, and

Ellie May had just found one final chocolate at the bottom of the wardrobe.

'It's been very nice staying here,' she said thoughtfully, 'but maybe next time we could go somewhere a tiny bit less splendid and not quite so marvellous. For example, I probably don't need to have three televisions.'

'I agree,' said Jeffrey. 'In fact, I'm rather looking forward to not having a television in my room at all!'

'Let's not get silly,' said Ellie May quickly. 'But, anyway, bye-bye, New York! You were really fun. See you soon.' She pressed the button for the lift. 'When do you think we can come back again?'

'You haven't left yet,' said Jeffrey. 'Why are you planning on coming straight back?'

'To see Zack,' explained Ellie May. 'Because I passed my second audition to be his friend and he's going to teach me how to sing and dance to a professional Broadway standard. He said to warn you that it could take a very long time.'

'Zack really is quite something, isn't he?' sighed Jeffrey.

'That song he sang in his show,' said Ellie May, 'about climbing up a ladder. I want to be like that when I sing high notes. You know, nice to listen to.'

'He is talented,' admitted Jeffrey.

'I'd have been terrified,' said Ellie May, 'doing all that stuff in front of so many people, but he didn't even seem to notice.' They stepped into the lift and the doors closed soundlessly behind them.

Jeffrey cleared his throat. 'Actually, I suppose I can tell you now. It was sort of a secret, but Zack's not –'

Ellie May held up her hand.

'Hold on,' she said. 'Is it a proper secret? The kind that you make a promise to keep?'

'Yes,' said Jeffrey, 'but –'

'No,' said Ellie May. 'Don't tell me. Because honestly, I don't think I'm massively good at keeping secrets. So it's probably better for me not to know.'

Jeffrey nodded. 'All right then,' he said. The lift doors opened and they stepped out into the hotel lobby.

Ah, the lobby of The Hotel Splendido Marvellousa! Ellie May knew that she would miss the doorman, in his top hat and long, flappy coat. She'd miss the spectacular flower arrangements covered in living butterflies. She'd definitely miss the heaps of ripe fruit, the bowls of delicious sweets, the fanned-out newspapers and magazines that lay upon the counter . . .

A headline caught Ellie May's eye:

CASSIE CRAVEN'S INCREDIBLE WEEK

The shy superstar breaks her silence exclusively to *Giggle*!

Ellie May grabbed Jeffrey's hand. 'Come on, let's go.'

'Yes, let's get out of here,' said Jeffrey. 'If I see one more celebrity magazine . . .'

'What?' said Ellie May. 'No, Jeffrey, I don't think you understand. I don't want to go *home*. I want to go and find a reporter. Because my week has been incredible too. Everyone will want to read all about it. Won't they? Jeffrey? Jeffrey, come back! Are you listening to me? Jeffrey . . . !'

The End

Ellie May Hits The High Note!

● ● ● ● ● ● ● ● ● ● ● ● ● ● ● ● ● ● ● ●

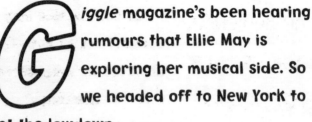

*G*iggle magazine's been hearing rumours that Ellie May is exploring her musical side. So we headed off to New York to get the lowdown.

'It's true,' laughed Ellie May. 'My album's out really soon and it's amazingly amazing!'

The album is called *I'm Zack* and it'll be released in April. 'Some people have said that it's really Zack's album,' the glamorous young starlet explained, over fudge cake and a side order of fudge cake. 'But I'm on two of the tracks. I play the triangle on "Broadway Way".

And if you listen really carefully at the end of "Ladder to Dreamland" you can hear me cough. It's a live recording, you see, and I was in the audience, choking on a pretzel.'

❝ I was in the audience, choking on a pretzel ❞

Of course, Ellie May couldn't have made *I'm Zack* alone. 'Kiko wrote three of the songs,' she told us. 'And Katsu recorded the backing vocals. I had some wonderful input from my chaperone, Jeffrey. And also Zack was there.'

We've been listening to *I'm Zack* here at Giggle Towers all week, and we just know it's going to be huge.

Now turn to page 34 for six superstar looks that'll have YOU dancing in the street!

_

Dinner Menu
THE HOTEL SPLENDIDO MARVELLOUSA

Starter
'Spud Jeffrey'
a jacket potato topped with curly kale

Main
'Supreme of Zack'
pan-fried starling

served with

'Ellie May Tomatoes'
grilled tomatoes in a hot fudge sauce

Dessert
'Kiko Surprise'
we are not allowed to tell you anything about this

sorry

_

Marianne Levy

Before she started writing books, Marianne was an actress. Not the incredibly famous sort, though. After graduating from Cambridge University she appeared in a few TV shows and did a bit of comedy on Radio 4. She has been in one film, in which she managed to forget both her lines. Since then, Marianne has written for *The Story of Tracy Beaker*, introduced *America's Next Top Model* and been the voice of a yogurt. She lives in London, and spends her spare time eating cheese and hassling other people's dogs. For news and fun stuff and to see Marianne reading extracts from Ellie May, visit **www.mariannelevy.com**

Ali Pye

Ali has always wanted to illustrate books, apart from a short time when she was seven-and-a-half and decided that she'd make a good police-dog handler. Luckily for the Alsations of Great Britain, Ali stuck (sort of) to plan A and eventually achieved her ambition. On the way, Ali studied fashion communication (this was part of the 'sort of'), which is very useful now she's drawing Ellie May's amazing outfits. Ali lives in London with her husband and children. Her favourite things are Arctic foxes, Chinese food and wearing too much eyeliner. You can see some early sketches of Ellie May at Ali's website, **www.alipye.com**

Laugh until you wobble at **www.jellypiecentral.co.uk**

Starring NOW in a
bookshop near you . . .